Green Eggs and Ham

By Dr. Seuss

HarperCollins *Children's Books*

17 19 20 18 16

ISBN-13: 978-0-00-715846-1
ISBN-10: 0-00-715846-7

© 1960, 1988 by Dr. Seuss Enterprises, L.P.
All Rights Reserved
A Beginner Book published by arrangement with
Random House Inc., New York, USA
First published in the UK 1962
This edition published in the UK 2003 by
HarperCollins*Children's Books*,
a division of HarperCollins*Publishers* Ltd
77-85 Fulham Palace Road
London W6 8JB

Visit our website at:
www.harpercollins.co.uk

Printed and bound in Hong Kong

That Sam-I-am!
That Sam-I-am!
I do not like
that Sam-I-am!

Do you like
green eggs and ham?

I do not like them,
Sam-I-am.
I do not like
green eggs and ham.

Would you like them
here or there?

I would not like them
here or there.
I would not like them
anywhere.
I do not like
green eggs and ham.
I do not like them,
Sam-I-am.

Would you like them
in a house?
Would you like them
with a mouse?

I do not like them
in a house.
I do not like them
with a mouse.
I do not like them
here or there.
I do not like them
anywhere.
I do not like green eggs and ham.
I do not like them, Sam-I-am.

Would you eat them
in a box?
Would you eat them
with a fox?

Not in a box.

Not with a fox.

Not in a house.

Not with a mouse.

I would not eat them here or there.

I would not eat them anywhere.

I would not eat green eggs and ham.

I do not like them, Sam-I-am.

Would you? Could you?

In a car?

Eat them! Eat them!

Here they are.

I would not,
could not,
in a car.

You may like them.
You will see.
You may like them
in a tree!

I would not, could not in a tree.
Not in a car! You let me be.

I do not like them in a box.

I do not like them with a fox.

I do not like them in a house.

I do not like them with a mouse.

I do not like them here or there.

I do not like them anywhere.

I do not like green eggs and ham.

I do not like them, Sam-I-am.

A train! A train!
A train! A train!
Could you, would you,
on a train?

Not on a train! Not in a tree!
Not in a car! Sam! Let me be!

I would not, could not, in a box.
I could not, would not, with a fox.
I will not eat them with a mouse.
I will not eat them in a house.
I will not eat them here or there.
I will not eat them anywhere.
I do not eat green eggs and ham.
I do not like them, Sam-I-am.

Say!

In the dark?

Here in the dark!

Would you, could you, in the dark?

I would not, could not,
in the dark.

Would you, could you,
in the rain?

I would not, could not, in the rain.

Not in the dark. Not on a train.

Not in a car. Not in a tree.

I do not like them, Sam, you see.

Not in a house. Not in a box.

Not with a mouse. Not with a fox.

I will not eat them here or there.

I do not like them anywhere!

You do not like
green eggs and ham?

I do not
like them,
Sam-I-am.

Could you, would you,
with a goat?

I would not,
could not,
with a goat!

Would you, could you,
on a boat?

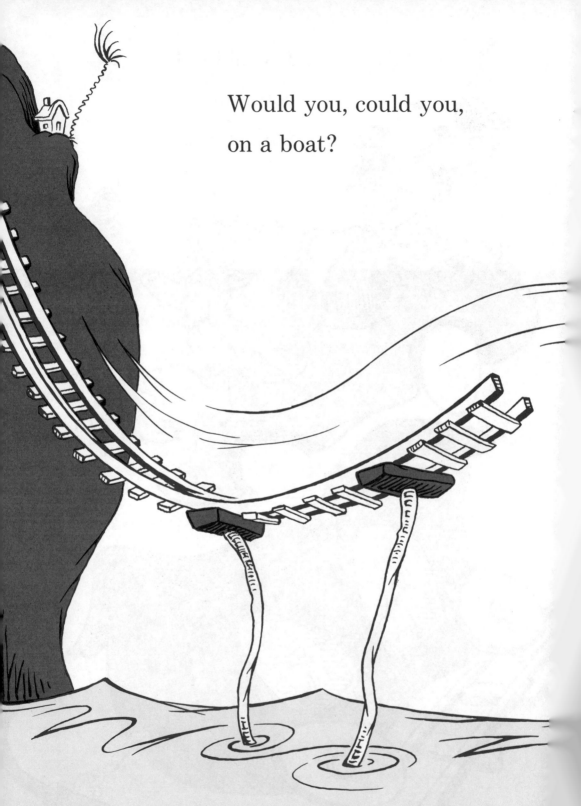

I could not, would not, on a boat.

I will not, will not, with a goat.

I will not eat them in the rain.

I will not eat them on a train.

Not in the dark! Not in a tree!

Not in a car! You let me be!

I do not like them in a box.

I do not like them with a fox.

I will not eat them in a house.

I do not like them with a mouse.

I do not like them here or there.

I do not like them ANYWHERE!

47

I do not like
green eggs
and ham!

I do not like them,
Sam-I-am.

You do not like them.

So you say.

Try them! Try them!

And you may.

Try them and you may, I say.

Sam!

If you will let me be,

I will try them.

You will see.

Sam!

I like green eggs and ham!

I do! I like them, Sam-I-am!

And I would eat them in a boat.

And I would eat them with a goat . . .

And I will eat them in the rain.

And in the dark. And on a train.

And in a car. And in a tree.

They are so good, so good, you see!

So I will eat them in a box.

And I will eat them with a fox.

And I will eat them in a house.

And I will eat them with a mouse.

And I will eat them here and there.

I will eat them ANYWHERE!

I do so like

green eggs and ham!

Thank you!

Thank you,

Sam-I-am!

Dr.Seuss™

The more that you **read**,
the more things **you** will know.
The more that you **learn**,
the **more** places you'll go!

– I Can Read With My Eyes Shut!

With over **35 paperbacks to collect** there's a book for all ages and reading abilities, and now there's never been a better time to have **fun** with **Dr.Seuss!**
Simply collect 5 tokens from the back of each Dr.Seuss book and send in for your

FREE Dr.Seuss poster

(rrp £3.99)

Send your 5 tokens and a completed voucher to:
Dr. Seuss poster offer, PO Box 142, Horsham, UK, RH13 5FJ (UK residents only)

Title: Mr ☐   Mrs ☐   Miss ☐   Ms ☐

First Name:.. Surname:..

Address:...

Post Code:............................... E-Mail Address:...

Date of Birth:............................ Signature of parent/guardian:......................

TICK HERE IF YOU DO NOT WISH TO RECEIVE FURTHER INFORMATION ABOUT CHILDREN'S BOOKS ☐

Read them **together**, read them **alone**, read them **aloud** and make **reading fun!**
With over **30 wacky stories** to choose from, now it's **easier** than **ever** to find the
right **Dr. Seuss** books for your child – just let the **back cover colour** guide you!

Blue back books
for sharing with your child

Dr. Seuss' ABC
The Foot Book
Hop on Pop
Mr. Brown Can Moo! Can You?
One Fish, Two Fish, Red Fish, Blue Fish
There's a Wocket in my Pocket!

Green back books
for children just beginning to read on their own

And to Think That I Saw It on Mulberry Street
The Cat in the Hat
The Cat in the Hat Comes Back
Fox in Socks
Green Eggs and Ham
I Can Read With My Eyes Shut!
I Wish That I Had Duck Feet
Marvin K. Mooney Will You Please Go Now!
Oh, Say Can You Say?
Oh, the Thinks You Can Think!
Ten Apples Up on Top
Wacky Wednesday
Hunches in Bunches
Happy Birthday to YOU

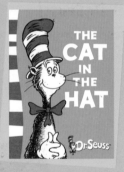

Yellow back books
for fluent readers to enjoy

Daisy-Head Mayzie
Did I Ever Tell You How Lucky You Are?
Dr. Seuss' Sleep Book
Horton Hatches the Egg
Horton Hears a Who!
How the Grinch Stole Christmas!
If I Ran the Circus
If I Ran the Zoo
I Had Trouble in Getting to Solla Sollew
The Lorax
Oh, the Places You'll Go!
On Beyond Zebra
Scrambled Eggs Super!
The Sneetches and other stories
Thidwick the Big-Hearted Moose
Yertle the Turtle and other stories